THE
Goblin
AND THE
Empty Chair

THE Goblin
AND THE
Empty Chair

MEM FOX & LEO & DIANE DILLON

BEACH LANE BOOKS • New York London Toronto Sydney

BEACH LANE BOOKS

An imprint of Simon & Schuster Children's Publishing Division

1230 Avenue of the Americas, New York, New York 10020

Text copyright © 2009 by Mem Fox

Illustrations copyright © 2009 by Leo Dillon and Diane Dillon

BEACH LANE BOOKS is a trademark of Simon & Schuster, Inc.

For information about special discounts for bulk purchases, please contact Simon & Schuster Special Sales

at 1-866-506-1949 or business@simonandschuster.com.

The Simon & Schuster Speakers Bureau can bring authors to your live event. For more information

or to book an event, contact the Simon & Schuster Speakers Bureau at 1-866-248-3049

or visit our website at www.simonspeakers.com.

Book design by Leo and Diane Dillon and Lauren Rille

The text for this book is set in Centaur.

The illustrations for this book are rendered in ink and watercolor on watercolor paper.

The borders are in colored pencil.

Manufactured in the United States of America

First Edition

10 9 8 7 6 5 4 3 2 1

Library of Congress Cataloging-in-Publication Data

Fox, Mem, 1946–

The goblin and the empty chair / Mem Fox ; illustrated by Leo and Diane Dillon. — 1st ed.

p. cm.

Summary: A goblin who for many years has been hiding himself

so that he does not frighten anyone finally finds a family.

ISBN: 978-1-4169-8585-3 (hardcover : alk. paper)

[1. Goblins—Fiction. 2. Self-perception—Fiction.] I. Dillon, Diane, ill. II. Dillon, Leo, ill.

III. Title.

PZ7.F8373Go 2009

[E]—dc22

2008041862

For Murray and Ruth—M. F.

For Anne and Allyn,
and to seeing true beauty—L. D. & D. D.

IN A TIME LONG PAST, in a land far away, there lived
a goblin who had once seen himself reflected in a still pond.

His reflection had frightened him so much, he decided to hide his face from the world forever, so as not to frighten anyone else.

He kept himself to himself,
took care not to be seen, and spent many years alone.

But one day, the goblin happened to see a farmer sigh,
set down his tools, and bury his head in his hands.

That night, the goblin went to work. He dug where digging was needed. He chopped where chopping was needed.

He painted where painting was needed.
And was careful not to be seen.

But in spite of his care, the goblin *was* seen.
The farmer, unable to sleep, stared out into the dark,
and watched without a word.

The following day, on the very same farm,
the goblin saw a woman sigh,
set down her pail, and bury her head in her hands.

That night, the goblin went to work.
He watered where watering was needed.
He planted where planting was needed.

He pruned where pruning was needed.
And was careful not to be seen.

But in spite of his care, the goblin *was* seen.
The woman, unable to sleep, stared out into the dark,
and watched without a word.

The following day, on the very same farm,
the goblin saw a child sigh,
set down her book, and bury her head in her hands.

That night, the goblin went to work.

He sat where sitting was needed.

He soothed where soothing was needed.

He stayed where staying was needed.
And was careful not to be seen.

But in spite of his care, the goblin *was* seen.
The child woke, kept very still, and watched without a word.

In the morning, the child, the woman, and the farmer sat silent at their table, staring at the chair that had been empty all winter.

Finally the woman set a place in front of the empty chair.

The farmer filled a plate with food.

The child opened the door.

And they waited.

The goblin waited too, and longed to join them.
But he dared not show his face,
lest it should frighten them away.

So he stayed where he was.

At last the farmer sighed and rose from the table without a word.
The woman followed, and the child made to follow as well.

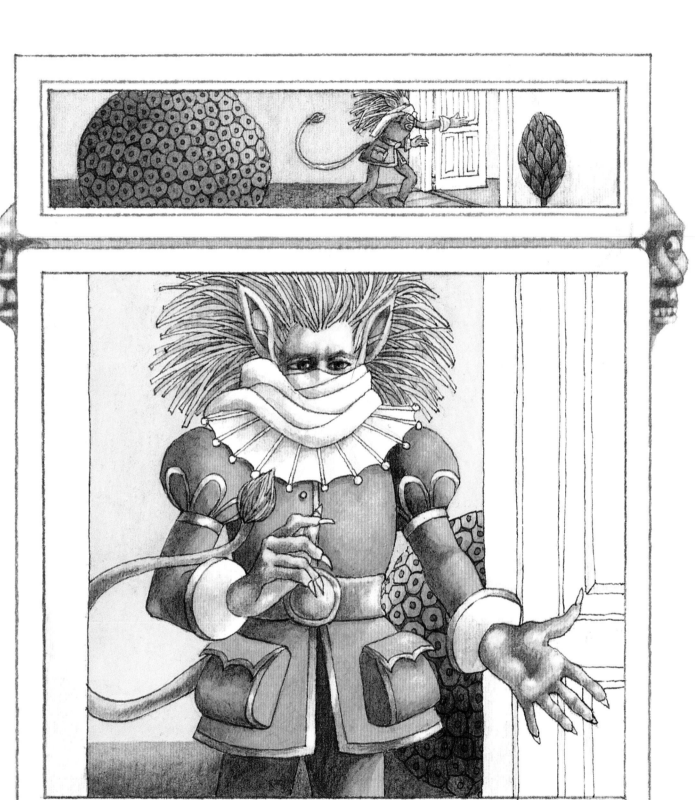

"Wait," said the goblin. "Wait."

So the farmer and the woman and the child sat down again.
And the goblin came and sat in the empty chair.

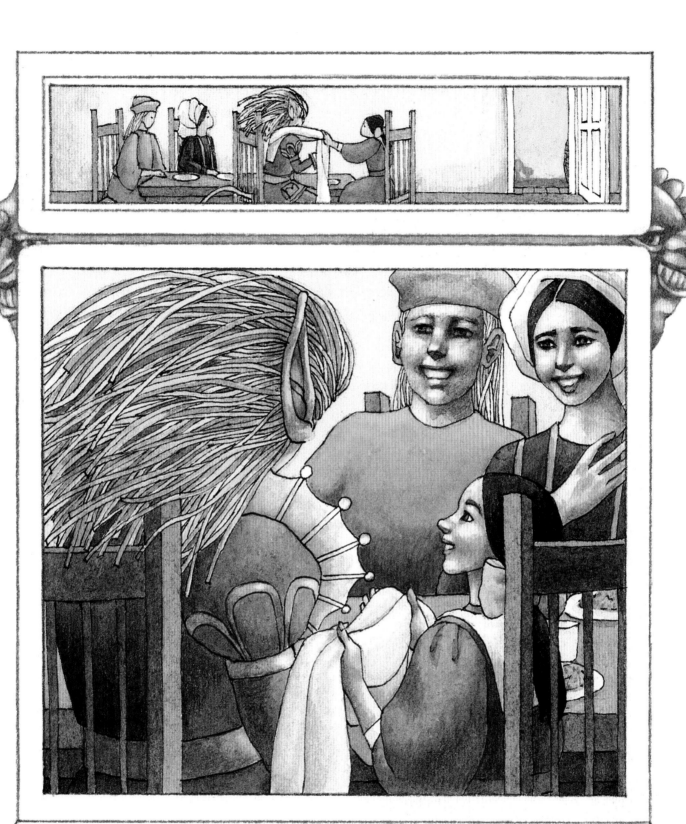

They looked at one another and smiled.

And they began to eat.